THE CRY IN THE FOREST

Kristien De Wulf

Illustrated by Elizabeth Catherine Vaughn

AuthorHouse™ UK Ltd.
500 Avebury Boulevard
Central Milton Keynes, MK9 2BE
www.authorhouse.co.uk
Phone: 08001974150

This book is a work of fiction. People, places, events, and situations are the product of the author's imagination. Any resemblance to actual persons, living or dead, or historical events, is purely coincidental.

© 2011. Kristien De Wulf. All rights reserved

No part of this book may be reproduced, stored in a retrieval system, or transmitted by any means without the written permission of the author.

First published by AuthorHouse 05/10/2011

ISBN: 978-1-4567-8008-1 (sc)
ISBN:978-1-4567-8009-8 (e)

This book is printed on acid-free paper.

For Robin, Louisa and Maxim

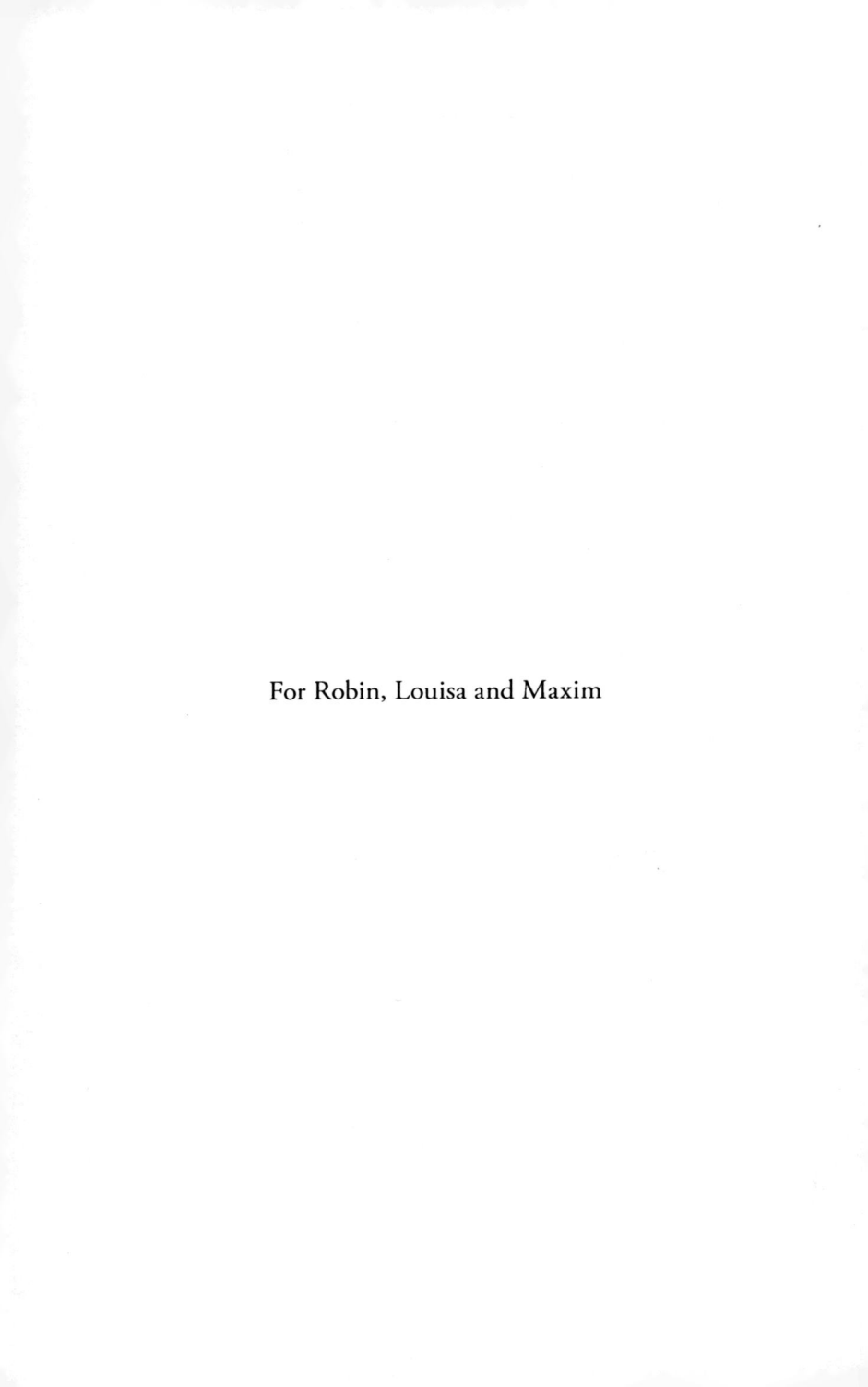

CHAPTER 1

"Hurry up, Jason. The taxi is waiting!"

"Where are the passports? They were here just a minute ago." Jason looks around the dimly lit hallway. His sister Emily is opening the front door.

"I've got them. Should we call Anne to see if she can bring an extra torch? I feel really bad about us leaving without one."

"No, it's okay. We can probably find one at the airport. Let's go."

The taxi driver places the luggage, one rucksack each, in the boot. Their parents follow them outside. Emily and Jason had said goodbye to them the previous night but even so they still got up early in the morning and couldn't resist making breakfast and bombarding them with well-meant advice.

"Please try not to fight the next seven days. Be polite to Phil's dad; he's ever so brave to take you guys along on a trip. Drink plenty of water, use sunscreen; Malaysia is even hotter than Hong Kong."

"Okay," Jason replies "and surely we're not supposed to talk to strangers?"

"And we must look after our belongings." Emily cheekily adds. "Don't worry, mum and dad, I'm fourteen now, remember. I'll look after my little brother."

"You're only invited because Phil's my friend," Jason sneers and then quickly opens the taxi door for his sister when he sees his mum's face change into a sorrowful grimace.

On the way to the airport Emily does a mental check of what she has packed, and hopes everyone will arrive on time. Phil's dad, who is a travel writer, got commissioned with the unforgiving task of writing a book for young travellers. He asked his son for suggestions, and then decided he would take Phil and his best friends along to put matters into practice. It hadn't taken the five of them long to choose the destination; Johor Bahru in Malaysia. Phil, a biologist in the making, was the keenest on visiting that part of the world as, according to him, the wildlife is absolutely fascinating. He'd already shown them various pictures of monitor lizards and snakes during break times in school. Emily is excited to see the eagles. She found out that the wingspan of the female White Belly Sea Eagle can reach up to two metres. Now, that is something that intrigued her. The way they dive into the sea to catch fish must be a magnificent sight.

In a different part of Hong Kong, close to Victoria Harbour, several flats are lit up. In one of them, a Chinese boy called Phu looks at himself in the mirror. The sleepless nights of the past couple of weeks are taking their toll. He looks older than his thirteen years and is not so sure about this holiday any more. He sighs. A daunting task awaits him. Why does he find it so hard to talk to his best friends? They need to know. The doctor warned him that the seizures can happen at any time. He mustn't go swimming by himself and must remember to take his medication regularly. On top of that, the doctor said that his friends should know about the recovery position. How easy he made it seem. Juvenile epilepsy. Phu looked it up on the Internet and read that epilepsy can develop in any person at any age. Half to two percent of people will develop epilepsy during their lifetime. Yeah, right, and he has to be one of them!

A sudden noise interrupts his thinking. The house cat, Feline, spins herself around his left leg. He strokes her tenderly. He takes his toothbrush from the basin and puts it in a small plastic bag. That's it; he's ready. Reluctantly he pushes Feline aside, picks up his holdall and camera and shuts the door behind him.

CHAPTER 2

Anne smiles and looks at Phil who is sitting beside her. The noise of the engine is quieter now; the ascent must be over. Five hours from Hong Kong to Senai and a one-hour drive to Buaya Sangkut. She picks up the travel guide and shows it to him.

"What do you make of this?" she asks. "A couple of years ago, there were claimed sightings of 'Orang Mawas', Malaysia's version of 'Bigfoot'. Whether it is true or not remains to be seen but research is underway to determine its existence."

Phil's attention is immediately drawn. "Oh, that's a very fascinating story. The rainforest in Malaysia is so big that some of it has never been fully explored. The locals have this myth that there are hairy creatures living there. Not quite apes as they stand on two legs. But, on the other hand, they are too tall to be human beings. The adults are more than three metres tall. They call them 'Orang Mawas', which means 'people of illusion'."

"You say 'myth', you don't believe it's true? Why would they make it up?"

"People like stories and using their imagination, I guess, but who knows, our campsite is the ideal location to bump into one of these creatures," he adds with a smile.

Johor Bahru is in the south of the Malay Peninsula. It is the most densely populated and vibrant region in the area. It is connected to Singapore by a causeway and bridge.

The Cry In The Forest

Travellers like to explore Johor's abundant natural charms. From Mersing, a fishing village on the east coast, local sailors can take visitors to the beautiful islands scattered throughout the aquamarine waters. Further inland, hikers can explore some of the last undisturbed parts of the rainforest in the Endau-Rompin National Park, named after the Endau and Rompin rivers.

There are four campsites within the park and chalets at the park headquarters. Tempted by promises of extensive palm species, pebbly beaches and large rivers with amazingly clear water, the five friends opted to stay in one of the smaller campsites there.

"Ladies and gentlemen, boys and girls; Senai International Airport has given us permission to land in ten minutes. The temperature on the ground is 28° C, humidity 78%. We hope you will enjoy your stay in Malaysia."

Emily glances out of the window. She can see the ocean and then the beauty of the coastline, a narrow strip of sand flanked by an abundance of trees. She ties back her brown, curly hair and smiles at her brother. "This is going to be a great holiday. I can't wait to sleep in a tent again. Let's cook something for Phil's dad tonight."

Jason keeps quiet. His head is spinning and the thought of food makes him quiver.

The taxi ride to their campsite is bumpy and uncomfortable.

"You're looking very pale, Jason," Phu points out.

"It must be the heat," Jason mutters. He doesn't usually travel in the summer and has a preference for cooler climates.

"We're nearly there. Hey, a signpost in English!" Anne is surprised.

"What, you didn't brush up on your Malay? I was counting on you." Phil likes to tease her and usually gets

The Cry In The Forest

away with it, apart from the one time when it all got out of hand and she caused an explosion in the science lab. How was he supposed to know that she would follow his homemade recipe for disaster to the letter? He'd got a serious telling off from the headmaster; and worst of all, Anne had made him sing in a karaoke bar in front of the whole class.

The campsite is small; about fifteen tents are spread out over an area of two hundred square metres. At first, Jason is all geared up to explore the surrounding area, but after putting up his tent he feels exhausted and plans to take a nap in the shade. The three boys are sharing one tent and Emily and Anne are together in the other one. Phil's dad decided to camp further away to give the children some feeling of independence and more importantly himself some peace and quiet.

The view is extraordinary; so many shades of green against an azure-blue sky. The cicadas are very loud, but the sound is so monotonous that Jason falls asleep within minutes.

"Mr Wells, shall we do a barbecue tonight?" Emily asks.

"Call me Roger, a barbecue sounds great. The nearest shop is a twenty-minute walk from here, at the next campsite. I'll heat up some water for tea. Phil, get me the gas stove, will you."

"It's not busy here at all," says Anne. "I suppose not having any electricity or hot water keeps the masses away."

"Well, I have work to do; you won't get to see me much this week. I'm sure you know how to keep yourselves occupied. Let me know if Jason gets worse. It might just be the long journey that makes him feel unwell."

Phil follows his dad, carrying the gas stove. "Are you sure you want to be on your own, dad?" he asks. "We don't mind your company."

"Thanks, son, but it's okay. I'll come and find you when I run out of ideas."

"We'll see you for dinner tonight then." But his dad is already rummaging through his rucksack, looking for a teabag. When Phil walks back to his friends, he hears thunder in the distance and dark clouds gradually cover up the sky. He looks at the surrounding tents and one stands out immediately. The colour is faded and it is patched up in several places.

"Hey Phil!" Phu shouts. "Can you give me a hand digging a trench round the tents? It looks like we're in for some heavy rain."

"That's a good start," Anne says and within minutes buckets of rain splash down on the tents.

CHAPTER 3

Half an hour later the rain stops. Emily looks for her suncream and mosquito repellent. "Who wants to go for a walk? Perhaps we can find our tour guide and confirm our hike for tomorrow?" Their Malaysian guide is called Dennis. They had booked him after several recommendations from tourist offices in Hong Kong. His knowledge of the rainforest is vast and he is in great demand. Nevertheless, he still lives in a typical Malaysian hut, close to his beloved trees and animals, and he ventures out everyday to count the nests of the birds or follow the tarantulas' behaviour.

Phu jumps up. "I'm coming with you." The two set off together. "Are you hungry, Emily? I didn't eat much on the plane. What time is it now, anyway?"

Emily smiles. "Let's go and find the shop after we've seen Dennis. We have to buy loads of food."

On the way out of the campsite they see a bunch of teenagers who are clearly Australians; a gold and green flag is posted near their tent. One of them is heating water to wash the dishes.

"Hi there," he calls out. "Just arrived? Come and meet the three of us."

"Hi; nice to meet you. I'm Emily; this is Phu. My brother, Jason, is resting there and Phil and Anne are right beside him. How long have you been here?"

"I'm Josh; these guys are Patrick and Steve. We arrived two days ago. It's an amazing place; we've seen so much wildlife in this short time. Look, there is a colugo sleeping in that tree. Night time is even better. If you go on a night walk, you can see some of the nocturnal animals like owls, bats or flying squirrels. Beware of the big bad wolf though, or rather ape," he adds with a cheeky grin.

"Yeah, right, we're on our way to the shop; let's talk later," Phu says, eager to continue walking. He turns around and sees Patrick and Steve steal a secretive glance at Emily. He immediately dislikes them both and hopes they will keep their distance.

The walk is a steep climb, not made any easier by the sultry humidity. Both Emily and Phu are feeling happy and sprightly, impressed by the palm forest. Emily suddenly gasps. In the distance she sees the Buaya Sangkut waterfalls. Phu grabs her hand and they stop for a minute to appreciate the breathtaking view. The forty metre long falls seem like static pools of water tumbling down into rugged boulders.

"I would love to go swimming," Emily says. "Let's ask the guide if it's safe around here."

"Sure. Look! That might be the hut where Dennis lives. It fits exactly the description we were given back home." The house is a typical Malaysian wooden structure with stilts below and palm leaves functioning as a roof. The vividly painted red stairs leading up to the main entrance make it stand out. They leave the trail and walk towards the house.

As there is no bell Phu shouts, "Hello, is anybody home?"

A middle-aged man with dark skin and long hair tied back in a ponytail appears from behind the pineapple plants in the garden.

"Good afternoon. I'm Dennis. Welcome to Malaysia." His smile is huge and there is a twinkle in his dark brown eyes. "Did you have a good flight?"

"Yes, thanks. I'm Phu and this is Emily. We'd like to ask you some questions about our walk tomorrow, hmm… if this is convenient for you."

"Please come in for tea, then I can tell you all about the walks we will be doing together."

Phu and Emily follow him into the house. It is small but very appealing. The walls are covered with batik paintings of turtles, eagles and flowers in vivid colours. Dennis brings them some cold lemongrass tea which tastes delicious and is very refreshing. He gives them a map and indicates where the first hike will leave from.

"Tomorrow we will leave early. I'd like to take you for a three-hour walk round the forest. Bring a swimsuit and towel and a snack. We should be back in time to have lunch at the campsite. Do you have experience in trekking?"

"Limited, I would say. We did the popular hikes in Hong Kong. But I guess you can't compare that to what lies ahead of us here," Emily replies.

"Well, trekking in Malaysia is a rich and rewarding experience. The weather is also going to be good; no more thunderstorms are expected for this week. We will pass the waterfall that you saw on the way here. According to the Orang Asli, the indigenous people, washing your eyes in the waterfall will save you from ever going blind."

"It sounds like you'll have some great stories for us. I can't wait," says Phu enthusiastically. "But now we have to head over to the shop. Thank you for the tea."

The Cry In The Forest

The shop at the other campsite sells plenty of local delicacies. They have a good look around and buy all that is needed for the barbecue.

"Emily, I'm glad you're here. I mean, I like this place and being here with Phil and Jason but I couldn't believe my luck when Phil told me you and Ann were coming along." Phu is worried that he said too much. He is suddenly shy. Luckily they're walking so he has a good excuse to look at the path. The seconds before Emily replies feel like hours. Eventually he plucks up his courage and looks at her.

"Let's race back to the others," she says with a big smile and starts running.

CHAPTER 4

Jason wakes up with a headache. He is obviously not coping very well with the heat. The cool airflow from the constant air-conditioning at home and in school feels a million years away.

"Hey, guys; I'm going to take it easy this morning and stay here. I don't think I can handle a three-hour walk right now. Take some pictures for me, will you."

He makes himself comfortable in his sleeping bag while Phu and Phil get ready for breakfast. In the meantime, Anne is boiling water for coffee and tea. There had been a nice selection of teas in the local shop and the bread rolls they had bought the day before are hugely appealing. They are all very hungry and enjoy the morning air with its damp smell of forest.

Half an hour later Dennis joins them and they are on their way.

"What a shame Jason couldn't come along. I hope he feels better this afternoon," Anne sighs.

"Oh yeah, he's not usually sick for very long," his sister replies. "Before we know it he'll be up and running like a madman."

They hear a rustling sound in the trees. At least four macaque monkeys, one with a baby, are right beside them. The baby is orange and clings to its mummy's belly. They stare at the humans and then nimbly jump from one tree to the next.

"They are so cute," Emily says. "I feel so lucky to see them."

"Yes," Dennis agrees. "And look there; don't move." He points towards a small light-green snake, about two metres away. Only an experienced eye could have spotted the viper, which rapidly disappears behind a tree.

They continue walking for about two hours while Dennis tells them many interesting facts, until they reach a large river. A side trail takes them to a deep, shady pool offering the refreshing swim they were waiting for. Enormous umbrella palms provide some welcoming shade as they head back to camp.

"Hi Jason; sleepyhead. Did you have a nice rest?"

Phu opens the tent and looks around disapprovingly. "Were you looking for something?"

Jason reluctantly lifts his head. "No, why?" Then he stops and looks at the mess in the tent. One bag is upside down, the contents spread out over Phil's sleeping bag. Another holdall is slightly torn and equally bereft of its belongings. A slight uneasiness comes over both boys as they realise that someone has been in their tent while Jason was asleep. He is wide awake now and looks around.

"Someone took my sunglasses," he shouts angrily, after frantically searching through all the luggage. He puts the clothes, towels and toiletries on one side of the tent. "Where is Phil? Maybe he has an idea of what's going on here." Jason's hair is dishevelled when he peers out of the tent. Phil, Anne and Emily stare sombrely at him.

Phu breaks the silence. "Perhaps we should ask our Australian neighbours if they saw something."

The campsite looks deserted. The only noise they hear is the sound of the jungle. In the distance they recognise a lonely figure, walking towards the main entrance of the camp, where drinking water can be obtained from a faucet.

Phu approaches the Australian boy and reluctantly talks to him about the apparent theft of their belongings from their tent. Josh drinks from his water bottle and frowns. His blue eyes look very serious.

"We were all out swimming this morning, so, no we haven't seen anything. There is something else though. Last night we saw a shadow moving outside our tent. Patrick saw it first and panicked so he woke us up. It was huge. The thing is, we don't think it was an animal as it was walking on two legs. It stayed for a couple of minutes, walking so close to us we could almost touch it and before we had the chance to look outside it was gone. I don't want to scare you, especially as you're here with some young ladies, but I thought you should know."

Phu breaks out in a sweat. "What do you mean, it was huge? Was it bigger than you? Bigger than an adult human being? Are you sure that's what you saw?"

"Absolutely positive," Josh answers. "Have you heard of *Bigfoot* or the *Yeti*? There is a myth that a similar giant, hairy creature lives in this rainforest. No one has found any real proof, but there have been quite a few reliable sightings."

Phu is now feeling faint and all colour has drained from his face.

"Are you all right?" Josh mutters anxiously.

"Yes, yes. I'll go and tell the others." Phu also realises he has to get to his medication quickly, or risks having a seizure. He tries to focus as he walks back to the others.

"There is something going on here. Josh just told me that some strange animal came sniffing round their tent last night. This might have something to do with our break-in. It looks as though it was some kind of ape!"

"Is that what Josh said? Wow! That's amazing! What if this is for real? We could actually see an Orang Mawa here." Phil's enthusiasm is not convincing anyone else.

"I'd rather not have them snooping around my tent, if possible. Let's tell Roger and perhaps also Dennis. He might know more about this," says Emily. "What about tonight; what if this Orang Mawa comes back?"

"I think we should talk to the other campers here," says an anxious Anne. "There are two more tents close to ours. Perhaps they know something and if they don't, we have to warn them."

"I'll come with you," says Phil eagerly. "I want to hear more about this creature."

Phu takes the pills he needs and is determined to explain his recent dizzy spells to his friends. He makes a mental note to do it that very evening and sets off to talk to Dennis and buy some food, after they have all agreed on what to have for dinner on their second night. Emily decides to stay behind. When Phu looks back he can see that she is talking animatedly to Josh, which dampens his mood.

Sometimes he wishes Emily was a little bird that he could put in a cage. He would listen to it singing and admire its beautiful colours. Some days he would let it fly freely in his bedroom, but it would be his, his only. But people aren't like that. They don't want to be caged. He has to find a way to get her to notice him.

CHAPTER 5

The tent nearest to theirs is occupied by two middle-aged Western men. It turns out they are here on a mission. They work for the World Land Trust, a UK based charity, helping to save endangered species and their habitats. The tallest one has greyish hair and looks very intelligent. Anne tries to show some interest in what they're doing and before long, the men explain the reason for their stay.

"The problem here is the incursion of oil-palm plantations. These plantations are very damaging as the soil is starved of nutrients, and after about twenty-five years nothing will grow, except grass."

"Not ideal for wildlife," adds his companion, a stout man with a very red face. "We are doing some research here but tell me, how can we help?"

Phil recounts what has happened so far, but the gentlemen are not impressed. "So, a pair of glasses has gone missing and someone saw a silhouette in the dark? Hmm, not done much travelling yet, have we?" the tall one mockingly observes. Anne nudges Phil and they walk towards the last tent.

"Look at that," Anne says with a grimace on her face. The tent has seen better days. "I wonder who's staying here," whispers Anne.

"Let's come back later," Phil suggests. "The other tents are quite far away. They wouldn't have heard or seen anything."

"What else do you know about these Orang Mawas, Phil? Do they attack people?"

"I don't think so, not without a reason. Don't let your imagination run wild. Nothing is certain. There is no reason to think they actually were at the campsite."

"Hmm, some funny characters camping out here, don't you think?" But Phil's mind has wandered off. He is trying to remember if there was anything in the article about the food preferences of the Orang Mawas, or if there was anything else he could lure them back with, if they were real.

Jason is tidying up the tent. Emily offers to make him some tea and he gladly accepts. Currently, they're all sitting outside on a rug waiting for Phu. The sun sets early here. Roger came by briefly and explained he had to miss out on the walk because of his troublesome knees. He went back to his tent after reassuring them that he's never heard of animals attacking people on a campsite.

"Let's play cards," suggests Jason. The others eagerly join in. They play a game called 'spades', which is a trick-taking card game played with two sets of partners. At the beginning of each round the players declare the number of tricks they believe they can take based on the cards in their hand.

Meanwhile, deep in the forest, Phu quickens his pace. It is getting darker, so he is grateful when he sees a light about twenty metres off the track. He thought it would be easy to find Dennis' house, but in the twilight distances are hard to measure. He shifts the weight of the bag, filled with groceries, to his left hand and switches on his torch. The path is overgrown and somehow seems different from the day before. It is much steeper; he is almost running out of breath going uphill now. He feels raindrops tickling his bare arms and realises that this is not where Dennis lives.

The Cry In The Forest

He turns his head and looks back. He is surrounded by the darkness of the jungle and knows that in a couple of minutes a curtain of rain will block his view completely.

The house in front of him beckons. Phu knocks on the door and a young Malaysian woman answers. She looks beautiful in her traditional dress. She smiles. Phu explains in English that he'd like some cover from the rain, but soon finds out that she doesn't understand a word of what he says. It doesn't matter as she leads him into the main area and points to a chair for him to sit on. Phu looks around; the house is almost empty. But then something catches his eye. On a small wooden table he sees a pair of sunglasses, very similar to the pair that Jason was wearing during the ride from the airport.

What a coincidence, he thinks and smiles at the young lady.

At the campsite Emily is getting worried. She is in the tent with Anne, listening to the heavy patter of rain. "Just what we need! Phu is not back yet and we can't even go and look for him in this weather."

"Well, I'm sure he's just taking shelter somewhere safe," Anne replies. "Perhaps he's with Dennis, or he might still be in the shop. There's no reason to worry. Soon the rain will stop and we can all have our dinner. I'm starving."

"Do you remember that time when your dog ran off and we went looking for it in the heavy rain?"

"Of course, but he was just a puppy at the time and didn't know our house that well yet. He was all right, wasn't he? Had a bit of a cold afterwards; hopefully Phu won't catch a cold."

"The funny thing was that we found him right opposite the butcher's."

"Yes, says a lot about him, doesn't it. My little dog is always hungry." Anne can talk endlessly about her dog. She teaches him lots of tricks and loves bathing him.

"I would like to have a dog but my parents are not keen. My favourite is a Labrador," Emily says. They carry on chatting and finish a packet of biscuits.

CHAPTER 6

Phu has another sip of the lukewarm tea the lady has given him and feels sleepy. The chair is comfortable, the atmosphere pleasant and although he feels reluctant to close his eyes in this unfamiliar house, he is unable to resist.

He wakes up with a slight headache and wonders where he is. It takes a while before he can adjust to the darkness of the room. A pair of dark eyes is staring at him. The size of the creature in front of him makes his heart skip a beat. He is too scared to say anything. Instead he looks around and then realises he is surrounded by at least three giants in a cave-like dwelling. One of them seems to be female; he can make out the shape of her breasts. They are not wearing clothes and are covered in hair, like apes. Phu remembers an image from his biology book about the evolution of the human being. The flat face, shortened jaw and long arms remind him of that picture; only these hominids must be nearly three metres tall. The strong animal scent makes him feel very sick. A noise on the right hand side startles him. He vaguely recognises the lady from the house where he had sheltered and then loses consciousness.

The rain had stopped nearly half an hour ago. Phu is still not back at the campsite. During the night Roger and Phil had gone to Dennis' house who told them there was nothing they could do in the dark. They had to be patient and wait. Finally the first rays of sunlight fiund their way through the trees. After a restless night the friends are tired and hungry, but above all worried about Phu.

"Let's split up in groups," Jason decides. "Anne and I will go out on a search with Dennis. Roger, you may want to stay here in case Phu turns up. Phil and Emily, you could have a look at the other campsite. We could really do with a mobile phone now. What a shame there is no network in the jungle."

Phil tries to think of a way to divert Emily, who is on the verge of crying. "I took some great pictures of the monkeys this morning. Would you like to have a look at them?"

"Okay, why not; you always were a great photographer. Your portrait project was one of the best this year."

"Thank you, but now I'm all into animals, although I do have the odd one with you in it."

At a different location, Phu comes to and the first thing he notices is the bad smell. It reminds him of his first school trip. They'd gone to a farm in the New Territories. It was the first time he saw pigs and wild boar being bred in an enclosure and the stench was unbearable. Some kids didn't mind and enjoyed the mud. Phu was amazed to see that some of his classmates were fascinated by chickens and geese. By the end of the day, Phu was convinced he'd never want to live near a farm. Fish are his passion. His dad had taught him early on how to use a rod, which baits to choose and even how to prepare the freshly caught fish.

An English accent brings him back to reality. "You're awake. How are you feeling? We don't want to frighten you."

"Where am I, who are you, what am I doing here?" Phu rambles on, relieved to see a human face and even better, someone who can speak English. He remembers now why he panicked and fainted. Three pairs of dark eyes are staring at him. The giants make some animal grunting sounds and leave the cave. They move very fast on their big feet, slightly hunched forward, their long hairy arms almost touching the floor.

"My name is Pete. You've met June", Phu follows his gaze and sees the young Malaysian lady. "We brought you here in a boat. We had to sedate you as this place is secret and we want to keep it that way. I know you have lots of questions. I can tell you one thing. The hairy people you saw will not hurt you. Don't be frightened. However, do not startle them. They are naturally curious like us, but have strong animal instincts. When you scare them, they will get angry and might attack. It's fairly straightforward. Don't throw anything at them and don't point a weapon or stick at them. Now, the good news; you have been brought here and can thus observe first hand how these exotic – some would say mythical - creatures live. You will be safe as long as you follow the rules."

Phu's throat is dry. "Why am I here? When are you taking me back to my friends?"

His initial relief at hearing an English speaking voice is gradually replaced by uncertainty. The prospect of spending more time here with these unfamiliar people is daunting. Phu is not the adventurous type and he wishes he was at home, in his bedroom, listening to music on the computer. These thoughts suddenly make him feel better again. June offers him a plate of freshly cut fruit.

"The reason you're here is a lucky coincidence for us," Pete continues. "Let me start from the beginning. Seven years ago I was working as a chemist for a big pharmaceutical company in Zurich. I was part of a team investigating the benefits of South Asian plants in medication; combining Chinese and Western medicine, as it were. That research brought me to Malaysia. One particular plant that I had read about caught my attention. It's a rare species. Quite by accident, one of my teammates and I came across it whilst we were exploring the Johor jungle a year later. It's an exceptional plant with huge benefits for mankind. However, during one of my expeditions I discovered something else; something just as important, or even more so, my instincts told me. It was this cave."

Phu looks around. There is a glow of natural light in the cave now. He realises he has spent the whole night away from his friends. This thought gives him hope. Surely they will be worried by now and start looking for him. He eats some of the pineapple.

Pete cherishes having an audience. "To cut a long story short, I knew this cave was inhabited. There were leaves on the floor outlining a sleeping area. I saw wooden and stone utensils and some fruit and nuts were stored away in the corner. At first, I thought the cave must belong to the Orang Asli, the indigenous people who live in the jungle. I was curious and hid behind some trees from where I could see the entrance. A couple of hours later my patience was rewarded. The three ape-like creatures you met appeared. They saw me, of course, but didn't attack. They were cautious but at the same time drew me in, as if they needed me. I have been their friend ever since.

A couple of weeks ago, a tragedy happened. Their only child fell ill. One morning his parents found him covered in sweat, moaning and shivering. He didn't eat anything for several days. By then their trust in me had grown so strong that they let me examine him. I have a lot of scientific equipment here so I made a diagnosis. You are the only one who can help him, Phu. When you were still at June's house, we took the liberty of searching through your wallet for your passport and health card. You're a perfect match. You have the blood group that we were looking for."

Further downstream, at the edge of the forest, the tents form a picture of colourful triangles. From a distance the area looks peaceful and serene. In reality though, emotions are running high. Emily is in tears. "I should never have let him go by himself."

Dennis is with them and consoles her. "We'll give it a couple more hours before calling the police; it is not so uncommon for someone to get lost in the jungle. People do find their way back thanks to the rivers. If he follows the river downstream, he is bound to find the campsite. I guess he took shelter from the rain and is now waiting for the sun to rise before venturing out."

Jason and Phil are restless. They want to search the jungle, but Dennis tells them there is no point going further than the surrounding area.

"Howdee!" Josh and Patrick are smiling, totally unaware yet of what had happened. Jason gives them an update of the situation and Josh comes up with a plan. "Okay, so if we can't go looking for Phu what about going for a swim? It will take your minds off him for a little while and there is no point in all of us hanging around here."

"Yes, why not? Come on. I'm getting fed up with sitting here." Emily grabs Anne's arm and pulls her up.

As it is the boys' turn to take care of dinner, Jason and Phil stay behind.

"Let's see if there is anything at all in the tent that can give us a clue. Have you noticed how quiet Phu has been since we left Hong Kong?"

"Jason, Phu is always quiet. I haven't noticed anything peculiar at all. Do you think we should call his parents, or is it okay to wait a little longer?"

"Better wait; you know what his mum is like. Well, any mum would freak out, I guess, but she is very protective of her son. The other day I called to see if he could come to the cinema and he wasn't allowed as it was a late night movie. Come on, the guy is thirteen!"

"Maybe they react like that because he's their only child. In my family, with five children, my parents don't have a clue about who's coming or going. My mum often complains that she never knows how many people will be around for dinner. Once there were two boyfriends and a girlfriend staying..."

The boys talk and cook for almost an hour. Dinner is nearly ready.

"Phil, don't you think it's strange that the only thing missing from here is the sunglasses? I mean, there is money here, expensive binoculars, my camera. It's still here, nicely tucked away among my socks. Why did the thief only take my sunglasses? It isn't even an expensive pair."

"Maybe you were waking up and he had to get out quickly. Luckily, he didn't harm you. Why are the girls not back yet? It's been ages."

Emily is slightly sunburnt but feeling much happier after the swim. They had a lot of fun in the water. Josh was very playful and they had a water fight with her on Josh's shoulders and Anne on Patrick's. Anne and Patrick won as Patrick is massive, like a bear, but in a cuddly way.

The rest of the day goes by slowly without a sign of Phu.

Roger brings some biscuits which they eat sparingly. The Australians spend most of the evening with them, showing their creative side by coming up with lots of implausible reasons why Phu has not returned. In the end Dennis sends them back to their tent, reasoning that it would be better to get some sleep if they want to help out with the search planned for the following day.

CHAPTER 7

After the long night, dawn brings some relief. Emily looks out of the tent. Her eyes are red-rimmed and she looks exhausted. The early sunrays lift her spirits and she starts getting dressed for the search.

"Come on, Anne; let's get ready. I will be so happy to see Phu. We must find him today."

"Yes, I know, what an awful start to our holiday."

When they leave the tent a group of six is waiting for them to join in; Phil, Jason, Dennis and the three Australians. They carry backpacks and the look on their faces is very determined.

"We will find him," Josh says.

"Let's form two groups of three," Dennis continues. "Here is a map on which I have highlighted two different trails. We will meet after a three-hour walk, exchange experiences, continue the search if necessary and meet here at the campsite after another three-hour walk. Please stay on the path as much as possible. By all means stay together and check your rucksacks for necessities thoroughly. Take at least two litres of water. Mobile phones will, unfortunately, not work but I have radios that can be used to stay in touch."

Phu is feeling sick. He wants to get out of the cave and run. He is scared, scared of Pete and the prehistoric creatures, scared of dying in the jungle. He knows however, that he can only escape from this situation by thinking hard, drawing up a plan. Not strength, but intelligence will have to get him out of here, so he needs to be patient. He wonders whether he can befriend the cavemen like Pete did, gain their confidence and thus regain his freedom. Now that he has been told the full extent of Pete's plan, he knows his days are numbered. The ape-child has kidney failure and needs a transplant. Phu has the right blood type and tissue, which means that one of his kidneys has less chance of being rejected by the child's body. Phu would be a living donor and feel perfectly fine after the operation, according to Pete. June would help them find the right hospital and her expertise as a surgeon, together with Pete's scientific knowledge, will make this plan a success. Phu is very doubtful. He doesn't want to lose one of his kidneys, especially not in a hospital in Malaysia; most definitely not in the hands of some mad scientist and unintelligible surgeon he has just met and who happen to be his kidnappers. *Oh my; I have to get out of here and soon!* he thinks.

He checks his watch; midday. He is alone now but notices the shadow of the female giant outside the entrance of the cave. Is she standing guard? He looks around and makes a mental impression of everything he sees. There is not a lot he finds immediately useful. In the corner some eating utensils, mixing bowls and stones are neatly stacked in a row. Using the hand-made tools as a weapon he wouldn't last a second. Suddenly his eyes rest on a dark spot opposite the entrance. It looks like a hole. He gets up and shakes the stiffness from his legs. He slowly moves to the back of the cave, keeping an eye on the female guard. She doesn't move and looks the other way, apparently enthralled by what is happening outside the cave. Phu can see the hole more clearly now. It is too dark to see its depth so he stretches out his arm and feels nothing but the cooler air coming from deeper inside. He walks towards the main entrance, deliberately making some noise so he wouldn't startle the woman. He had read an article once about Bigfoot in North America. Not prone to believe anything without scientific proof, he'd put it aside. He wishes he'd paid more attention. He remembers that Bigfoot fell under the list of cryptids, meaning that its existence is suggested, but not necessarily proven. Other examples that cross his mind are dinosaurs (and who would doubt they existed) and also the okapi, which for a long time was regarded as a purely fictitious animal.

The woman turns her ape-like head towards him. Her expressionless eyes are set deep in the hairy face. Her nose is flat and wide, the lips and chin protruding farther than the nose, the neck absent. She towers high above him. Phu smiles while he tries to walk past her. She moves to the side leaving Phu to blink in the strong light. In front of him is a wide expanse of low-cut trees. The view reminds him of something he saw in a film about the sole survivor of a shipwreck on a deserted island. There is a man-made table with chairs; wooden poles bound together with rope. Above it is a leafy shelter to protect anyone sitting there from the sun and the rain. In the middle of the open space is a fireplace surrounded by stones. The smell of grilled fish is mouth-watering. Pete and June obviously had their say in domesticating these cavemen. Wild flowers adorn a small path that leads to a river. He can just make out the father and son who are bathing in the water.

"Hi Phu, how are you? Hungry?" Pete turns the fish around and looks invitingly at Phu. "Take a seat, lunch is nearly ready. Here are Jason's sunglasses. Adam took them during one of his expeditions. He can't help it; he loves our gadgets and accessories. Anything shiny or fancy, he'll bring it along. It is rare for me to be able to return one of his treasures."

June puts slices of banana and coconut on different leaves that are the size of small plates. Pete adds a piece of fish and it really looks like a meal fit for a king.

"I've named them Adam, Eve and Moses," Pete proudly remarks. "Adam is a very good fisherman; this is his catch. Do you like it?" Phu nods and realises it is actually quite delicious. The hairy giants feast on the fish and then disappear into the jungle.

"Moses looks cute," Phu whispers. He and Moses are the same size, even though Moses is only about five years old.

"I can tell his age from the way he is losing his milk teeth. Isn't it extraordinary how much they resemble us? Or should I say, 'we resemble them'. The only ability missing is speech. They don't seem to communicate much; they just follow certain patterns, a fixed routine."

"Where do they sleep?" Phu asks, eager to find out as much information as he can without sounding suspicious.

"Sometimes they sleep in the cave. When the night is dry and the moonlight strong, they don't sleep but go out exploring. They know it's safer for them to walk around during the night, especially now that the jungle is being exploited by innocent hikers, curious explorers and vicious businessmen alike. Not many of them have survived and they feel the threat of us humans.

The question remains: are they our predecessors or a different species closely related to us? I honestly can't say. I need more time. My resources here are limited. Luckily, I have my trustworthy, intelligent companion June. She and I and two other Malaysian experts are the only ones who know about their existence. If the secret comes out too early that will be the end for them. Ruthless scientists will keep them locked up like lab rats."

Tell me about it! Phu exhales deeply. He is not sure what to think of this conversation. He closes his eyes, hoping that when he opens them the reality will not seem so daunting.

"The issue of the 'missing link' is huge. The whole theory of evolution could be reversed, or finally proven beyond doubt." Pete is enjoying his speech with the energy of someone who is onto something big.

We're getting sidetracked, Phu thinks. "Has no one ever seen any traces of them?"

"Oh yes," Pete replies. "Footprints especially, that's why there is such a big interest in them now. The cave is off the beaten track, which speaks for itself. The jungle is so dense around here that the only way to get here is via the river."

Phu looks around eager to find out where they hide their boat. The sun is at its highest now, its burning rays turning the river into a glistening green lane meandering past their hidden oasis. The contrast between the vastness of the jungle and the triviality of a young man planning his escape is tremendous. Phu sighs. Is there any point in trying to escape?

CHAPTER 8

A kingfisher jitters and sets off, flying in a westerly direction, halting after a couple of minutes on the branch of a ramin tree.

"Yes, put a mark on that one. Lovely wood! Let's go back to the camp now. I'm thirsty but can't face another sip of water. A cool beer, that's what I want." The man, tired and hot, licks his lips and touches his moustache.

His Mexican friend adds, "We've marked two hundred and fifty trees, another fifty tomorrow and our job here is finished."

"Well, we've got to keep an eye on those cutters, you know, make sure it all gets loaded into the right truck. Did you know it will take six weeks by boat before the goods arrive in Europe?"

"Yeah, well, we should be home long before that. I don't like it here. Can't see why all these young people travel to this dump. Surely nowadays they can afford to stay in a nice hotel."

Less than half a mile away but invisible because of the dense undergrowth some of these young people are still looking for their friend.

Josh reaches out his hand to Emily and pulls her up a ridge. "We've nearly reached our meeting point. The others will soon be here. Maybe they will have some good news. How long have you all known each other?"

"I've known Phu for three years. Jason and I lived in Shanghai before we moved to Hong Kong. Phil, Phu and Anne have been in the same class for a long time. I immediately got on well with Anne. We're in the same netball team. You know what amazes me about Phu? He was actually very enthusiastic about coming on this trip. He is very shy and it takes a while before you get to know him, but it is worth the effort," she smiles. "He is one of the kindest people I know."

They climb the last stretch and then see the sign post that Dennis had indicated on the map. They are too tired to appreciate the beauty of the seaside view from their elevated position and sit down, sticky and hungry.

"I don't understand it." Emily's voice trembles. "Where can he be? It's not like Phu to wander off by himself. He doesn't even go out in Hong Kong without pressure from us."

Josh's friend, Patrick, has been quiet for a while. "I think we need to get the Malaysian authorities involved sooner rather than later," he finally says.

Josh is not convinced. "Dennis wants to wait until we get back this afternoon. Oh look, here they come."

The hope in his voice is soon gone when the other team arrives with Dennis following, all looking exhausted and no sign of Phu. Anne tries to shake off the feeling of gloom that settles on her.

Dennis is the first to speak. "Is everyone feeling all right? We'll have a half-hour break here and will then continue. Please look after yourselves and rest when needed. If there is no trace of Phu by the time we get back to the campsite, an official search team will go out. Don't worry too much about him. People are fairly inventive and resilient."

The Cry In The Forest

Phu looks up at the ape-boy who is standing right in front of him. He is feeling slightly nauseous as the boy is smelly and grunts like an animal. Moses then walks off towards the river and turns around, waiting for Phu to follow him. Phu gets up and walks down the path. He actually feels like swimming as well. He takes off his clothes and soon both of them are enjoying the lukewarm water.

Phu forgets all about his fear. The water rinses all his anxiety away and he smiles at his new-found friend, thinking what a pity it is that he can't talk.

Moses turns out to be a very good swimmer. He stays underwater for very long stretches and then reappears quite a distance away. Phu is understandably wary, remembering the doctor's orders. He stays close to the shore and will not go further than where he can stand. His feet touch the soft ground. He can see little grey fish shooting past. When Moses swims towards him, he starts a one-sided conversation.

"Hey Moses, you're like a dolphin. Do you want to know why I'm standing here? I have an illness. I'm not sick like you are. All my organs work but something happened to my brain. The connections between my brain cells are not always perfect. And when that happens I am in a different place and I can get hurt. So now you know; you're the first friend I'm telling this to. And do you know what? It feels great to tell someone. I could tell you anything."

Moses looks at him, disappears under water, and swims one more round. Then Phu follows him, away from the shore, head under water. He can't keep up with Moses, but he feels elated, swimming freely in the peaceful river.

When they are back on land, Moses and Phu sit at the edge of the river and Phu watches Moses catch some insects. No one else is in sight. Moses starts walking away and then waits for Phu. They go into the jungle and Phu's heart starts beating faster. *Where are we going?* And then he notices. In front of them is a swamp that leads to the river. A motorboat is hidden right there under the low-hanging branches.

Phu is shocked. *Why is he showing me this? Is he trying to help me?* He takes a closer look and knows he can steer this type of boat. Growing up in Hong Kong amidst a family of fishermen certainly comes in handy. He just needs to find the key to start the motor and then he can flee! He looks at Moses, filled with gratitude. On the way back to the cave he wonders whether Moses ever feels lonely.

Pete comes out of the cave and looks surprised to see them together. Phu quickly tells him about the swimming and asks how bad Moses' illness is. "What would happen if he didn't get a kidney transplant? Will he die?"

"That is hard to tell. He will definitely show some nasty symptoms soon. He's already got itching limbs and muscle cramps and occasionally vomits quite badly. That will get worse as the waste products in the body and the blood accumulate."

"And my body can function perfectly well with one kidney?"

"Yes, this kind of transplant is very common nowadays. Don't be frightened, the recovery is rapid and after a while you won't even notice that you only have one kidney. The danger for Moses is greater, as his body might reject the new kidney. But we should be hopeful. It is worth trying anyway."

Phu wonders if this is the scientist speaking, or the compassionate friend. Is this all just some kind of experiment for Pete, or does he honestly want to help this hairy youngster? At this moment Moses looks up towards him with his deep-set, dark eyes and in that short time when their eyes meet, Phu almost loses his will to escape. He is torn between his feelings of friendship for this fascinating creature and a sense of self-preservation. He starts to feel weak. Everything turns black and he falls down on the soft ground.

At the campsite the men from the World Land Trust are looking at the neighbouring tent with some suspicion. They have been sent here on a specific mission and presently think they may have reached a breakthrough. Over the past couple of days they have been keeping an eye on the two men with harsh features and rude manners who occupy the ramshackle tent. They hardly ever spoke, but a Spanish accent could be distinguished on the rare occasions they did.

"It's very quiet here today, isn't it? Where are all the young people?" the grey-haired man asks his companion.

"Apparently one of the boys didn't return to his tent last night. The lady in the shop told me they've gone out on a search for him. He bought some food and then probably lost his way after that. They haven't had much luck on their holiday yet. I hope he's all right."

"They must be so worried. I hope they find him quickly. We don't really want the police here, not yet. It'll scare our timber dealers off and then we have to start from scratch again. Any day now they'll start cutting the trees and we'll have the necessary proof. We have to catch them red-handed."

"Yes, I can't wait until another one bites the dust. I'm going to the shop to make a phone call. My family are waiting to hear from me. See you later." He puts on his hat and heads off, sweating and panting.

Josh is chatting away to Emily. She is enjoying his company and is happy that he can take the edge of her fear away. Josh is eighteen and talkative, the very antidote of shy and wistful Phu. The magic of the jungle is still there but now it feels as though it's full of hidden dangers, rather than interesting animals and perfect scenery. If only there was something else they could do to find Phu.

"Have you been to Malaysia before?" she asks.

"This is my third trip here, but my first time in Johor. I travelled with Patrick and Steve last year. The year before that, I went to Langkawi with another friend and his parents but they moved away and we rarely see each other. I know Malaysia quite well now. It's a lovely country. Next year I'd like to visit Borneo."

"I think I might just stay at home next year," Emily says with a little twinkle in her eye. She is convinced that everything will be all right soon. They are nearly at the end of the afternoon walk and everyone is talking about how the following day's search will be officially organised and therefore many more people will help looking, especially people who know the jungle and have experience in conducting searches.

Dennis, however, secretly wonders what the two men that he heard in the forest were talking about. Nobody could have missed their loud Spanish sounding voices. They couldn't be seen but Dennis knows their sort and what they're up to. Experience has taught him to stay out of it. He's a nature guide and the Malaysian police have warned him before that they don't like interference. It could cost him his job. Silence is golden.

CHAPTER 9

When Phu opens his eyes he is lying down with his head supported by June. Pete and Moses are standing next to him and in the distance he sees Adam and Eve.

"Hi Phu," Pete says. "Are you all right? Would you like some water?"

"Yes, please. I guess I fainted again?"

"Yes, is there something we should know?" Pete asks suspiciously. Moses' eyes are full of compassion.

"Yes," Phu sighs. "I have epilepsy. It is rather new for me as well. I got the first symptoms about five months ago. Luckily for me I was at home the first couple of times that I fainted. My parents took me to the hospital the first time it happened. I have my medication but everything is in the tent."

Pete is angry. "It's important that you tell us these things, Phu. We will perform an operation on you soon and even though you will be in the best possible care, we cannot take any unnecessary risks. We want everything to run as smoothly as possible so that we can save everyone involved and keep it secret. So if there is anything else you haven't told us, it is important that you tell us now. Also, we need to get hold of your pills as soon as possible. It is too risky to enter your tent during the night, as people are bound to be awake waiting for your return, so we will have to do it tomorrow while everyone is out looking for you."

"Everyone is looking for me?" Phu mumbles. This brings him back to reality.

"Can I come with you tomorrow?" He is desperate to see the campsite, even though no one will be there. "I'd like to bring some more of my stuff here."

"I don't think that is a good idea. Just tell me exactly where your pills are and I'll see what I can do about the other things."

It is getting darker now. June is preparing dinner and Adam is sharpening a kind of spear. Preparing for the hunt, Phu thinks. He wonders if Moses is also going on a hunting trip.

"When are you planning to carry out the operation?"

"We have an operating theatre booked for the day after tomorrow. If Moses is well enough we will perform the operation then."

Phu goes into the cave to think. He is on his own for a couple of minutes and then Moses comes in and sits opposite him. They look at each other for a long time and then Phu carefully reaches out his hand and strokes Moses' arm. The smell is not pleasant. He tries not to breathe through his nose, so as not to offend his new friend. His arm is soft as you would expect with all the hairs, and Moses' eyes lighten up after this sign of affection.

Phu's friends are having an equally hard time. Dennis explains the schedule for the following day since he is most accustomed to the area. Emily, Anne and Roger will stay at the campsite. Phil and Jason will join the fifty-odd people who have volunteered to continue the search. The volunteers are mostly Malaysian locals who have done this before.

"Nearly every year someone goes missing in the jungle," Dennis tries to reassure them. "So far everyone has been found. You will have to look for clues, such as clothing, dropped gear or ground marks. We will do a line search, which means that each searcher must be able to see all the ground between him and the next person. We will go off the track this time and penetrate deeper into the jungle."

Phil's feet are hurting. He has some big blisters but still, there is no way he could just sit there and wait. Any action would be better than doing nothing. He misses Phu and wishes there was more that he could do. He looks around. The campsite is busy at this time of the day. Some people are having a shower; others are cooking or sitting outside the tent, resting after a walk in the heat or a swimming session. When the middle-aged Englishmen got back to their tent and realised that Phu was still missing, they immediately came over and expressed their concern. They also asked whether the police would be involved. At least they show they care, Phil thought, which is more than can be said about the guys in the ramshackle tent. They haven't even said hello. Sometimes you wonder why people travel and camp. It's supposed to be social, isn't it?

Phil wakes up from his daydream when Dennis leaves.

"He's a nice guy," says Jason. "If only he'd given us some survival tips right from the start, such as where to find drinking water and edible plants. Do you think Phu knows about this kind of stuff?"

"Let's try to relax a little, Jason, there's nothing we can do until tomorrow."

The next morning Moses is the last one to wake up. Phu is sitting quietly next to him, studying his facial features, his long arms and legs and strong feet. Moses can stand upright in the cave but only just. If he keeps on growing at this rate, he will have to bend his head in a year's time. Phu holds his breath when he sees that Moses walks towards the dark hole that Phu discovered on his first day in the cave and disappears. He waits for a couple of seconds and then crawls after him into the hole. The only way to get his bearings is

The Cry In The Forest

by following Moses' grunting sounds. The ground scrapes off his knees and he is relieved when the tunnel becomes big enough to stand, with his head bent forwards. It is getting lighter now in the tunnel and Phu tries to look past Moses to what is in front of them. Above all he wants to ask him so many questions. Why is he showing him how to escape? Is he intelligent enough to understand what is happening? Does he feel sorry for Phu? The questions remain unanswered and Phu is truly mesmerised when he steps out of the tunnel into a smaller cave and from there back into the jungle.

He can't think clearly and feels hypnotised when he walks out into the sunlight. There it lies in front of him; a way out, a path to freedom. But something is holding him back. How can he thank his friend? How can he run away from someone who sacrifices his own life and relies on him for survival?

Moses doesn't stop though. He is already disappearing behind the big ramin trees that tower above them. Phu puts his thoughts aside and follows him as fast as he can. It is a lot harder for him. Moses, whose feet are big and strong after years of walking barefoot, is a lot more agile than his appearance would make one believe. Phu struggles to keep up with him. Suddenly he hears a loud bang. He sees Moses come to a halt. His hairy knees buckle and he keels over backwards. Moses' head hits a piece of wood. Phu runs towards him and kneels down beside him. "Moses," he whispers.

Moses opens his eyes and looks anxiously at Phu. A voice can be heard from behind the trees about twenty metres away. Someone is shouting in Spanish. Phu doesn't understand what they are saying and the voices become quieter and disappear altogether.

Moses is bleeding. He has a bullet wound in his right shoulder. Phu bends over and to his dismay sees that the blood at the back of his head is not from his shoulder. He must have hit his head on something very hard. Moses is wailing and Phu doesn't know what to do. He looks around and tries to think. His mind is racing.

He is too heavy for me to carry. I will have to get help. But how do I find my way back? Everything looks the same.

"Should we go and check what we shot at?" one of the Mexican men asks his companion. "Just to make sure it was an animal?"

"Of course it was an animal, what else would it be? Don't get all paranoid on me now. Let's finish here and go back. I've had enough of this place, too much going on. Brazil was easier."

He puts a yellow mark on a beautiful tree and the pair of them walk back to the campsite, ignorant of their misdeed.

Phu doesn't feel the pain when he hits another low-hanging branch. He feels very bad about leaving Moses behind, but knows there is no other way. He has to find the cave urgently. Luckily they hadn't gone too far yet. He spots the entrance to the tunnel and crawls back the same way they had come. Pete is just outside the cave, making some notes at the makeshift table. He looks angry. "Where have you been? We've been looking for you for the past half hour. Where is Moses? Was he with you?"

Phu inhales deeply. "He is wounded. He was shot."

"What do you mean, he was shot? Where is he? Who saw him?" Pete's anger turns into concern.

"Moses and I went for a walk. I mean, he took me somewhere. I think he wanted to show me something. Then suddenly I heard a bang and I saw him fall down. He has a wound in his shoulder and hit his head when falling. He is too weak to walk. He is bleeding a lot. You've got to come quickly."

June rushes to the boat to get the first-aid kit and they all crawl back into the tunnel.

"Goodness me! Moses took you through this tunnel? What on earth did he do that for? His parents are out looking for him too." Pete's voice sounds hollow.

Phu is surprised at how easy it is for him to find the same trail. Some kind of sixth sense leads him back to the spot where Moses is lying. He isn't moving at all. His eyes are wide open. The smell is nasty but Phu wants to touch him and hold him. June strokes him and calls out his name. No reply, nothing. She then checks his pulse. Nothing. June shakes her head. Phu feels terrible.

With a trembling voice Phu murmurs, "Is he dead?" The silence that follows is a brutal confirmation. He kneels down and caresses Moses. "I'm sorry," he says. "I should have looked after you."

"This is not your fault," says Pete, who has never looked more tense. "I can only hope it was a tragic accident and whoever shot at him thought he was aiming at an animal. If I find out who his killers are, they will not come off lightly. I'm sick of people carrying weapons and shooting mindlessly at animals. It's against the law and luckily the punishment is harsh in this country. Let's take Moses home and bring him to his parents. What a tragedy. Their only child."

June and Pete carry Moses. Phu can no longer hold back his tears. He feels guilty for even having contemplated running. If he is honest, right now he wants to stay with these new companions a little longer and comfort Adam and Eve in any way he can. Moreover, he wants to show Pete that he can be trusted and will not talk to anyone about this family when he goes home. *That is, if they will let me go.*

CHAPTER 10

Meanwhile, at the campsite, the Englishmen are ready to catch their prey. They've worked it all out. They've seen the trees that are marked for cutting, they know who the culprits are and now all that is left to do is inform the Malaysian police. Timing is all-important.

"All's well that ends well," the shorter one says. "My family can't wait to see me. They will be so proud when I tell them how we thwarted the plans of these ruthless timber dealers."

"Well, they won't have to wait long. Everything is set for tomorrow. Have you seen how many people left to look for that boy? Solidarity still has some meaning over here."

"That would be the same in England. In the countryside at least it would, perhaps not so much in a big city where everyone is minding their own business and running around trying to achieve something."

Adam and Eve are wailing. The noise is heartbreaking. Eve is lying down next to her son and Adam is pacing up and down. For Phu this is the worst scene he has ever witnessed. After a while June brings water for everyone. Pete cautiously touches Adam's arm and takes him to a flat area not far from the river. Adam nods knowingly and the two men start digging. This will be Moses' burial place. After they've finished, June puts flowers along the side in an inconspicuous way. To an outsider it doesn't look like a grave, which is how they want it.

Phu keeps quiet. It is Pete who makes the next decision.

"We will have to leave this site. It is too dangerous for us to stay here. Phu, I don't want to hold you captive for ever. You know how important it is that this all remains secret. Things have taken a very different turn from what we all thought. I can only hope that you don't betray us. In any case we will have gone by the time you reach the campsite. To give us more time I will tie you up to a tree. It should take you at least an hour to free yourself. Pete takes the rope that Adam is holding and pushes Phu towards the nearest tree."

Phu turns towards him. "Can I stay with you all a bit longer?" The question startles himself as much as June and Pete. "I would like to stay to grieve with you all. I really feel I need some time with Moses' parents to get over this. After all, Moses was my friend."

Eve looks at him with her dark eyes. Phu is not sure what to make of it. The eyes don't show the same emotions as a human face. She comes closer to him and then lifts him up in her arms as if he were a child. When she puts him back down again, a feeling of warmth stays with him.

"Phu, I'm sorry, but I can't allow this." Pete is adamant. "There is too much at stake. My assignment here has come to an end. I will shortly return to Switzerland and continue my research. I feel I have failed in one area but I strongly believe I can accomplish my goal in herbal medicine. The Orang Mawas don't need my help; actually, they might be better off without our interference. Adam and Eve are not alone here. Perhaps, one day, it will be accepted that there is more than one kind of human being but until that day they should be left in peace."

When Phu is tied to the tree they all leave and he wonders if he'll ever manage to free his body as the rope is so tight around his hands and feet he can't move anything. He is so engrossed in his task that he hasn't seen June entering the cave again. Everyone else has gone.

June appears from the cave with something in her hand. It is Jason's sunglasses and a small spear Moses has made. Phu starts crying when she puts them at his feet and loosens the knots a little.

It is evening when Phu reaches the campsite.

The search team has done their job to the best of their ability. There was huge disappointment when Dennis called it a day as there was still no sign of Phu.

Emily is sitting outside her tent. She looks up at the sound of footsteps coming closer. She can't believe her eyes when she recognises Phu's distinctive walk and stares at him. Her voice falters when she shouts his name.

"Hi Emily, I'm so glad to see you," Phu says.

Jason, Phil and Anne come out of the tents and they all hug each other.

"So, where have you been, buddy?" asks Phil. "Great to see you're safe and well."

"There is so much I have to tell you," Phu says hesitantly.

"I know," Emily replies. "We have all the time in the world. It's just so good to have you back."

"Go on, tell us what happened," Jason insists. Phu tells them the story he had made up on his way back. He'd got lost after buying groceries. After walking for hours he took shelter in a cave, ate some of the food he had bought and tried unsuccessfully to find his way back. Eventually, a Malaysian lady called June, found him.

Phil is suspicious. "Why did it take you so long to find us?"

Phu hesitates and then the words that he had wanted to say to them for so long come out. "I have epilepsy. I was unconscious when June found me. It is new for me too. Actually, having spent some time in a different environment made me see more clearly. It is not the end of the world. I guess the worst thing is that I can't drive or ride a motorbike."

"Oh, well, make sure you earn enough to afford a driver," Jason remarks.

Soon after, Roger and Dennis hear the good news and the search is called off. Night falls early. It is dark and serene until the Australians arrive. The group of youngsters chatter and laugh until the early hours.

The following morning the rain is back. The kind of warm, tropical rain that makes everyone feel happy and alive. Water everywhere, feeding the rainforest and its inhabitants.

"What is it, Phu?" asks Phil. "I think you haven't told us everything."

"If I tell you, I'll betray someone I care about very much. I need your help though. I want to go back into the forest."

"Okay, I'm dead curious but I'm not going to force you to tell me if you don't want to. We'll come with you. Whatever reason you have, it must be a very good one. This is just for a couple of hours, isn't it?"

"I think so. Thank you for coming along. I wouldn't be able to do this on my own."

"Do we need to bring anything in particular? I have a compass, a measuring can for the rain, a book about insects…"

"Ha, ha, no, just bring your usual self."

The Cry In The Forest

"Vete al Diablo!" A row erupts from behind them. Phil and Phu see two men with angry faces walking towards them. They finally get to meet the Mexicans, who are in a foul mood but stop fighting when they are standing face to face.

"Why all these people always here? What you do, walking or what?" one of them asks. His face is red and covered with wrinkles. Beads of sweat cover his forehead.

"Hmm, nice to meet you too," Phil answers. "Yes, we have been walking in the rainforest. I hope you're also enjoying your stay."

The men look anything but happy with their holiday.

"We don't want noisy here, before you come much better. If you come near tent, you will regret."

The other man looks even angrier.

"Idiota," he mumbles and he pulls his friend away.

"Okay, well, what have we not experienced during this holiday?" Phil says mockingly. "A threat was surely missing. As if we would want to go near their filthy tent!"

"Let's get ready for our jungle tour," says Phu.

CHAPTER 11

"Would anyone like more coffee?" Anne asks matter-of-factly. Her mind is in turmoil though. She can't believe what she has just heard. Phu, Emily and Phil have agreed to go back into the jungle for no plausible reason. Phu has some kind of unresolved issue there. "No offence, but would you not rather enjoy the beach for the next couple of days?" she adds.

"Anne, it's just something he wants to do. We will all be fine."

Phil, pragmatic as ever, sees no reason to discuss this any further. When a friend needs a favour, he complies; as long as it is within the boundaries of the law, of course. Anyway, he owes Phu a favour. When his gran died, three years previously, his mother was grieving so badly she couldn't take care of the household. Phu often invited him for tea at his house and helped him through this painful period. Whatever it is that makes Phu a different person, he wants to be there for him. He is also relieved to see that Emily is coming along. Phil doesn't like it one bit that she gets on so well with Josh. At least he will be out of the picture for a little while and she can rebuild her friendship with Phu.

While Ann and Jason are clearing the breakfast table, the three youngsters set off. Phu has told them that he wants to follow the river upstream. He hasn't said much more, partly because he doesn't know where to start. Above all, he is tired and sad. Phil and Emily are trying to lift his mood.

Their easy chatter distracts him and after a while he starts to talk.

"I met some other people in the jungle."

"Other people? What do you mean?"

"Okay, this is going to sound awkward. You know, those prehistoric look-alikes that we talked about on the first night here? Well, I saw them."

The sound of the cicadas is louder as they advance in the rainforest, or so it seems. Emily wipes her sweaty front with her sleeve. She is well covered to protect herself from insect bites.

"So, they are real! Where did you see them? Did they see you?"

"I lived with them."

"Wow, that's amazing! What are they like? They obviously didn't harm you," Phil says.

"Were you kidnapped?"

"Kind of, but not by the Orang Mawas; an English guy called Pete held me captive as he was interested in one of my kidneys. He wanted to do a transplant on one of the youngsters. The little boy died before the operation."

"So, where is this Pete now, is it him we're looking for? What about informing the police? Surely this is a crime they'd be interested in. Kidnapping a kid, he needs to be in jail."

"That's where the problem lies. If we tell the police I'd have to tell them about the ape people. I don't want to do that. They'll be hunted and exploited."

Phu explains further about his friendship with Moses and then tells them about the shooting accident. They reach the river after most of the story has been told.

"By boat it would take us about fifteen minutes to get to the cave. But since we have no boat, we will have to walk.

It might get pretty dense, but it is our best bet for finding the place."

"I'm still not really sure what you're looking for. I thought you said they will all have gone by now?" Emily tries to be patient and understanding, but the long walk in the heat is wearing her down.

Phil comes to the rescue. "We might just as well continue now that we're here. Let's get to the bottom of this. In the meantime, I have a question for you. Who can tell me the difference between jungle and rainforest? No answer? Okay, jungle applies to forest with dense undergrowth, the kind you have to use a machete to get through. In tropical rainforests, jungle only occurs at the edge of the forest, such as along rivers or in clearings where a huge tree has fallen. Basically, for jungle you need a lot of light coming through and in the rainforest the canopy prevents many plants from growing underneath."

"Thank you, Phil, for this piece of very useful information. Don't you all wish you were back at school? It definitely seems way easier than surviving here," says Phu.

They walk on in silence. Emily is a little upset as she can't find the right words to say to Phu. She feels he is slipping away and wonders if they'll ever feel the same about each other again. She moves closer to him.

"I missed you when you were gone, and I think you are very brave to tell us everything. We got to know the Australian guys a little better. Hmm... Anne and I went swimming with them and it was fun, but I'm so glad you are back."

"It's okay, Emily. Let's not talk about it now." Phu retreats into his own world again, with his own thoughts and Emily realises she will have to work harder to break through that barrier.

CHAPTER 12

The Mexicans are counting their blessings. Their job is almost done and the price of wood has risen. The boss is very happy and has offered a pay rise.

"When did the boss say the locals were meeting us?" one of them asks in heavily-accented Spanish.

"Any time between nine and ten this morning. Let's get going. This campsite is giving me the creeps. Too many kids here."

"Yeah, did you see that? One of them just got back and now he's gone off again with a rucksack and all sorts of gear. What's going on?"

"Kids looking for adventure. For us it is part of our daily life. As long as they mind their own business, they can have as much adventure as they want."

With smelly clothes, puffy eyes and forlorn faces they locate the meeting place on the map, take water bottles and a gun and set off for what they hope will be the last trek in the Johor jungle.

In the same jungle, within a reasonable distance, the Englishmen are lying in wait. They know from experience that there is a certain pattern that tree cutters follow. They've chosen a spot right at the beginning of the forest area and are accompanied by two armed Malaysian soldiers. Suddenly, they hear voices. Their binoculars aren't of much use as the path is winding. The soldiers raise their rifles in readiness. But then they relax; the people approaching them are teenagers, tourists enjoying a jungle tour on their own. The Englishmen leave their hiding place and greet them.

"Where are you off to today? You are very brave, trekking like that without a guide."

"We just can't get enough of the jungle!" Phu says sarcastically.

"Well, you be careful now. Don't hang around here. There are not many people passing here and the path gets increasingly rugged. If you turn right at the next intersection, you will get to a wider track with some interesting scenery. See you tonight at the campsite."

"Okay, 'bye then. Don't worry about us. Enjoy the rest of the day," Emily replies.

After a long and hazardous walk they reach the cave.

"Everything has gone!" Phu is slightly disappointed. "There used to be a table here and chairs and a pretty garden."

The cave is deserted and no clue has been left behind.

"I guess they're used to covering their tracks," Emily says. They stay near the spot where Moses is buried for a while and then decide to walk back.

Two pairs of eyes are watching their every move. As soon as the cave and its surrounding area are quiet, the tall and agile creatures run off. Their pace is swift, their faces grim. The male holds a spear, the female a piece of tree trunk. They track the scent of evil.

The Mexicans will never reach the meeting place. It's a quarter to ten. The killings are quick and virtually silent.

CHAPTER 13

Ann, Jason and Dennis are having tea when the Englishmen run across the campsite towards them. "Your friends are in danger. Some Malay soldiers are looking for them. Do you know the people who stayed in that tent over there? Two Mexicans, they were found dead this morning and it looks as though they were murdered."

"What? Murdered? What are you talking about? We've come here for a holiday and it looks more like we've landed in a viper's nest. Why are there soldiers here? Did you see our friends?" Jason's face is turning crimson.

"Why were the Mexicans murdered? Should we help trying to find…" Anne doesn't finish her sentence. She is relieved to see Emily, Phu and Phil at the edge of the campsite.

"Now that you are all here we can tell you a bit more about our job and why we are here. My name is Gerald and this is Frank. We told you before that we work for the World Land Trust, which is true, but we have a secondary, more secret task, in order to protect the environment. Over the past ten years we have successfully tracked down several groups of illegal tree cutters. Usually the locals fell the trees, but we are after the commissioner."

"That's right," Frank intervenes. "And this time we were onto something big but someone got in there first. The Mexicans were part of a huge organisation and it is a shame they are dead as we would have liked to get more information. Still, we are not totally sorry. They were vicious."

"But that doesn't give us an answer yet as to who might have killed them," says Jason, "and the murderer is still out there."

"Well, this is no longer in our hands. The army has taken control now and it wouldn't surprise me if they told us all to leave the premises early. If I were you, I'd pack my bags and go home sooner rather than later. That's what I'm going to do, for sure."

Frank acts upon his words and walks towards his tent, followed by Gerald who looks at them compassionately and recommends they check the flight times before setting off.

Phu closes his eyes. His body aches all over. He understands what has happened and feels empty inside. He looks at Emily and Phil for reassurance and they nod knowingly. They are just about to tell Ann and Jason what they know when they are interrupted once more.

"Hey guys, wanna come over for a farewell drink? We're flying home tonight," Patrick calls out.

"Sure, we'll be with you in a minute," Phil says. "Are you going to join us, Dennis?"

"No, I'm going home. I have some work to do. Prepare some walks for the next guests coming here. I do hope you'll come back here. You're great kids."

They shake hands and Phu wonders how much he knows but maybe Dennis wants to play it safe, as there is a lot at stake.

"When are you heading home? Shall we swap email addresses?" Josh looks at Emily but Phu grabs her hand and says, "You can have my email address. And you're very welcome to stay at my place if you visit Hong Kong."

They are having a good time considering the circumstances and stay until the Australians have to go to the airport.

"So, Emily, where would you like to go next for a holiday?" Phu smiles at her and he can't remember having ever felt so close to anybody.

And the Englishmen, well, they are looking for their binoculars, which seem to have gone missing from their tent.

EPILOGUE

Phu has made up his mind. He will study anthropology, the scientific study of the origin and behaviour of man. He wants to learn everything that has been written about this subject, but realises that some things will always remain a mystery.